THE GREAT SPACE RACE

Written by Ant Johnson   Illustrated by Ivan Allen

© Crystal Clear Publications Ltd   London

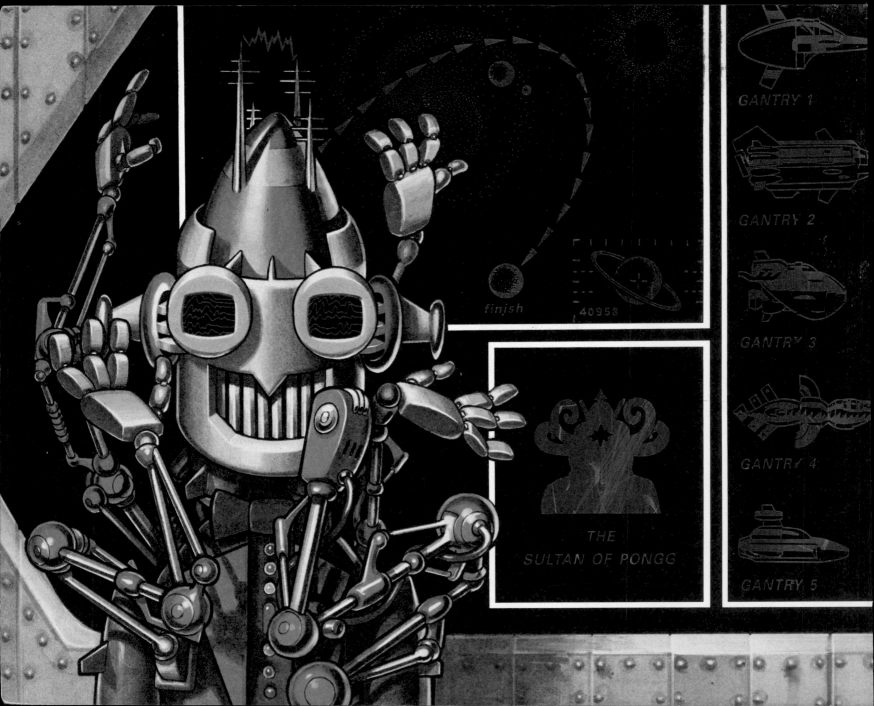

...IT'S ANOTHER FINE NIGHT HERE AT **ASTEROID TOWERS**. THE STARLIGHT IS FAIRLY BEATING DOWN UPON THE TRACK FOR A RACE THAT PROMISES TO BE A REAL NAIL BITER. STAY WITH ME – YOUR ROBOTIC COMMENTATOR **MIKE ROCHIP**, TO WATCH FIVE OF THE GREATEST GALACTIC SPACE PILOTS COMPETE FOR THE HAND IN MARRIAGE OF THE MYSTERIOUS **PRINCESS AMMONIA**...LET'S GO OVER TO THE DISTANT PLANET **LAVATORIAH,** TO HIS SUPERFLUOUSNESS THE **SULTAN OF PONGG** FOR SOME ROYAL OPENING WORDS...

..."LADYBEINGS, GENTLETHINGS, AND ALL THAT MOVES IN THE FIRMAMENT, TONIGHT IS A VERY SPECIAL NIGHT. SPECIAL BECAUSE ONLY ONE OF OUR FIVE RECKLESS SPACE HEROES WILL WIN THE HAND OF OUR FAIR DAUGHTER AND BECOME **'LORD OF THE BLACK HOLE'**. HOWEVER, ALL RUNNERS UP WHO COMPLETE THE COURSE WILL BE GIVEN THE CHANCE TO SPEND A DAY AT **THE CRUCIAL SOUNDS STUDIO** WITH THE **GALAXY'S** TOP ALIEN POP GROUP – **CULTURE SLUG**. THE FUTURE IS IN YOUR HANDS. **GO FORTH WITH THE GRACE OF PONGG!"**...

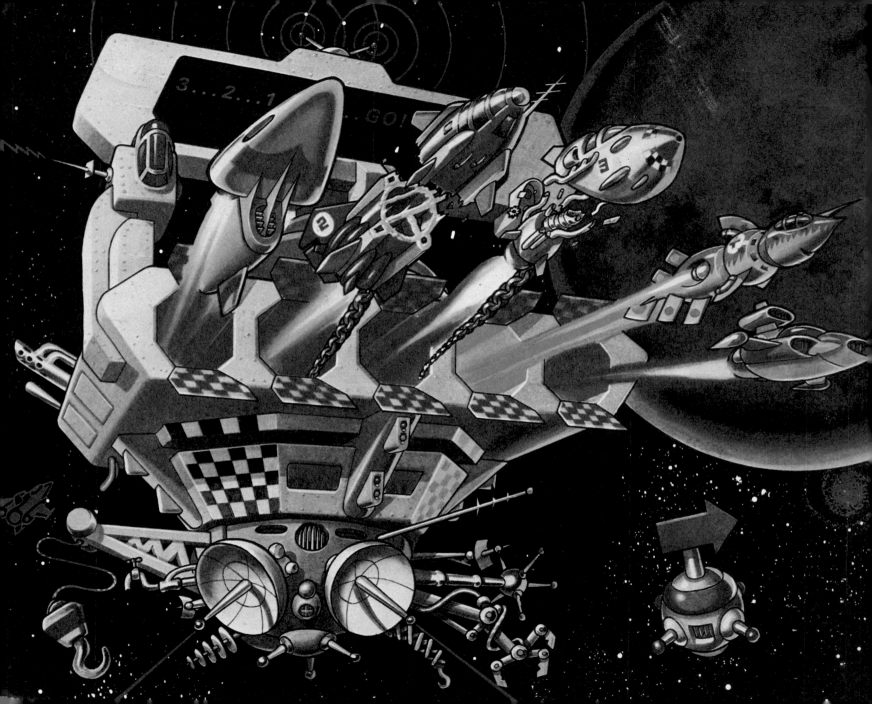

...THANK YOU, YOUR **MAGNITUDE**. I'M SURE OUR BRAVE PILOTS WILL APPRECIATE THOSE FINE WORDS OF ENCOURAGEMENT. AND NOW OVER TO THE **RACE STATION** TO TAKE A CLOSER LOOK AT TONIGHT'S LINEUP...

...IN GANTRY 1 WE HAVE ODDS-ON FAVOURITE EARTHMAN **JONNY FABULOUS**...IN GANTRY 2 – THE GREAT **ATOMIC PILE** IN HIS NEW EIGHT-CYLINDER TURBO NUCLEAR **ASTRO BLASTER** – NO SHORTAGE OF POWER HERE...IN GANTRY 3 WAITS **PRANG OF PLUTE**, FAMOUS FOR MORE THAN FIFTY COLLISIONS IN HIS RACING CAREER...IN GANTRY 4 IS COMMANDER **SPLUGG** FROM **JELLOTON**...LASTLY, AND YES, PERHAPS LEAST OF ALL IN GANTRY 5 IS **NEBULOUS THE NONENTITY**...WE WEREN'T SURE UNTIL LATE THIS AFTERNOON IF HE WAS GOING TO MATERIALIZE, BUT HE HAS FINALLY GOT HIMSELF TOGETHER AND CONVINCED THE LINEDROIDS THAT HE'LL KEEP HIS ATOMIC STRUCTURE STABLE ENOUGH FOR TONIGHT'S COURSE...

...THEY'RE UNDER STARTERS ORDERS...**5**...**4**...**3**...**2**...**1**... **THEY'RE OFF!** OH NO! SHIPS 2 AND 3 ARE BREAKING UP! WE'VE HARDLY STARTED AND WE'RE DOWN TO THREE SHIPS ALREADY...

...AS THE REMAINING RACERS APPROACH THE FIRST LAP IT'S EARTHMAN **JONNY FABULOUS** IN THE LEAD LOOKING TANNED AND RELAXED FROM HIS RECENT INTERPLANETARY CRUISE, CLOSELY FOLLOWED BY COMMANDER **SPLUGG**, WITH **NEBULOUS** TAKING UP THE REAR. **FABULOUS**, HANDSOME AND SHINING, IS SHOWING NO SIGN OF EASING THE PACE AT THIS EARLY STAGE OF THE RACE. HIS NEWLY INSTALLED ELECTRO-SCANNER KEENLY CHARTS THE EXACT POSITION OF HIS RIVALS AS HE CALMLY CONVERTS INTO DOUBLE LIGHT-SPEED...

...OH NO! HURTLING HELIOTROPES! **NEBULOUS** HAS ACCIDENTALLY DEMATERIALIZED AND IS TOTALLY OUT OF CONTROL. HOT DOGS AND ASTRO-SHAKES ARE FLOATING ABOUT EVERYWHERE...THE CROWD IS GOING WILD WITH EXCITEMENT AS **SPLUGG** OVERTAKES **JONNY** ON THE INSIDE LANE.

...COMMANDER **SPLUGG** IS RACING AHEAD...WILL THE **PRINCESS** MARRY THIS UGLY ALIEN? WE'RE JUST RECEIVING THE CLOSE-UPS OF **SPLUGG** ON CAMERA 5...YES WE HAVE HIM ON VISUAL – TIGHTLY GRIPPING THE CONTROLS OF HIS THIRD-HAND BARGAIN-BASEMENT **INSECTOPOD** – THE CABIN STEAMY WITH **SPLUGG** SWEAT AND HOT SLIME...LUST FOR VICTORY IS WRITTEN ALL OVER THE BITRI-FOCAL FACE...

...**SPLUGG** IS A PART TIME FASHION MODEL FOR '**ALIENS OWN**' AND WON THE TITLE – '**GOURMET OF THE GALAXY**' LAST YEAR, BAKING A RECORD THREE-TIER FUNGUS AND ANCHOVY PIZZA...

....THE TENSION IS MOUNTING...CAN **JONNY FABULOUS** REGAIN THE LEAD?...ANYTHING COULD HAPPEN IN THESE CLOSING MINUTES...

...WHAT'S HAPPENING NOW? IS **JONNY'S** SHIP BREAKING UP? NO...HE'S THROWING OUT EVERYTHING IN AN EFFORT TO REGAIN THE LEAD. EVERYTHING INCLUDING THE GOLD TAPPED WASH BASIN...OUT GOES HIS HALF POUND OF SHERBET ALIENS, HIS RUBBERIZED IN-FLIGHT UTILITY BATHING SUIT, AND HIS HAND-TOOLED LEATHER RAY-GUN BELT. BUT **SPLUGG** IS CLOSING IN ON **JONNY** FAST...CAN **JONNY** DO IT? IT'S NECK AND NECK HERE AT **ASTEROID TOWERS**. THE CROWD HAS REACHED FEVER PITCH WITH EXCITEMENT. AND YES IT'S **JONNY FABULOUS** – **JONNY FABULOUS** HAS WON THE RACE. **THREE MILLION CHEERS FOR JONNY!**

*...AS THE TWO SURVIVING RACERS BLAST DOWN UPON THE FINISHING PAD A CROWD OF **ROBOPOLICE** ARE SURROUNDING **JONNY'S** CRAFT. HAS HE BEEN ARRESTED? LET'S GO OVER TO OUR RACING EXPERT **ANTI STATIC** FOR AN UPDATE ON THE SITUATION...*

*...YES MIKE – IT LOOKS AS IF **JONNY** HAS BEEN OFFICIALLY DISQUALIFIED. HIS FINGERPRINTS HAVE BEEN FOUND ON THE CHAINS TIED TO SHIPS 2 AND 3...SINCE HE'S THE ONLY COMPETITOR WHO HAS FINGERS ANYWAY I THINK WE SHOULD HAVE SUSPECTED HIM A LOT SOONER...*

*...I THINK YOU'RE RIGHT **ANTI** – HE DOES LOOK A BIT SHIFTY. HIS EYES ARE FAR TOO CLOSE TOGETHER AND HE'S ONLY GOT TWO OF THEM ANYWAY. THE CROWD ARE ALL CHEERING **SPLUGG** NOW, AS HE IS GREETED BY THE FANTASTIC **PRINCESS AMMONIA** WITH A LARGE WET KISS.*
SIX MILLION CHEERS FOR COMMANDER SPLUGG!

...FOR THE DISQUALIFIED **FABULOUS** THERE'S CERTAINLY NO SUCH WELCOME. RADIO CONTROLLED **ROBOPOLICE** HAVE OUR CHEAT HANDCUFFED AND UNDER GUARD...

...YES **MIKE** I DON'T THINK THE CROWD THINK HE'S THAT FABULOUS ANYMORE AND I DOUBT VERY MUCH WHERE HE IS GOING, THAT HE'LL EVEN GET TO HEAR THE LATEST RECORDING BY **CULTURE SLUG**. LET'S HOPE THE **SULTAN OF PONGG** WILL SHOW SOME MERCY TO **JONNY**. THE LAST TIME A SPACE PILOT BROKE THE **GALACTIC CONVENTION** HE WAS CONVERTED INTO STRETCH COVERS FOR THE **SULTAN'S** THREE-PIECE SUITE...

...STAY TUNED VIEWERS ON THIS CHANNEL FOR THE ROYAL WEDDING, COMING UP AFTER THE COMMERCIAL BREAK...